Good Night, Baby Ruby

Rohan Henry

Abrams Books for Young Readers, New York

Artist's Note

I have always been a disciple of the master storytellers who were able to capture readers with timeless tales and illustrations that were expressive, meaningful, and simple all at the same time. Author-illustrators such as Shel Silverstein and Crockett Johnson are the first two that come to mind. When it came to illustrating the protagonist of *Good Night, Baby Ruby*, I tried to reveal the essence of a little girl who wants to explore the world around her, have fun, and put off bedtime for as long as possible!

Baby Ruby is based partly on my two-year-old daughter, but she is also inspired by the music of John Coltrane. I listened to Coltrane exhaustively while I illustrated this book. As I placed each image on the page, I was acutely aware of how the placement of each line would affect the mood and tone of the artwork in much the same way a chord or a musical note affects melody.

Library of Congress Cataloging-in-Publication Data

Henry, Rohan.
Good night, Baby Ruby / by Rohan Henry.
p. cm.
Summary: Baby Ruby does not want to go to bed, and despite the preparations her parents make at bedtime, she keeps hiding.
ISBN 978-0-8109-8323-6
[1. Bedtime—Fiction. 2. African Americans—Fiction.] I. Title.

PZ7.H3968Go 2009
[E]—dc22
2008024683

Printed and bound in China
10 9 8 7 6 5 4 3 2 1

Abrams Books for Young Readers are available at special discounts when purchased in quantity for premiums and promotions as well as fundraising or educational use. Special editions can also be created to specification. For details, contact specialmarkets@hnabooks.com or the address below.

HNA
harry n. abrams, inc.
a subsidiary of La Martinière Groupe

115 West 18th Street
New York, NY 10011
www.hnabooks.com

For Kaela, Ruby, and Honey B

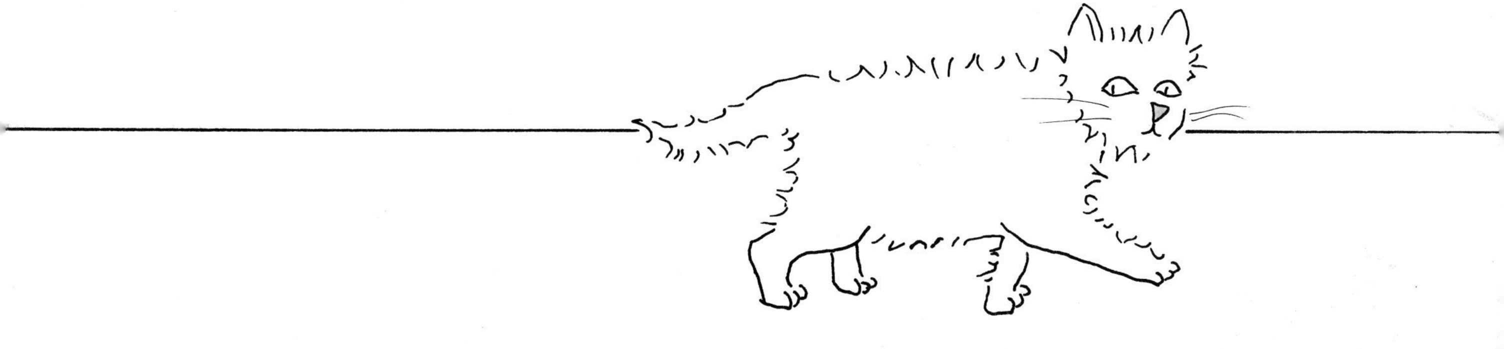

This is Ruby's Room . . .

but where is Ruby?

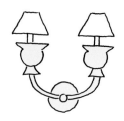

Here is Kitty! And here is Ruby . . .

She is in the bath.

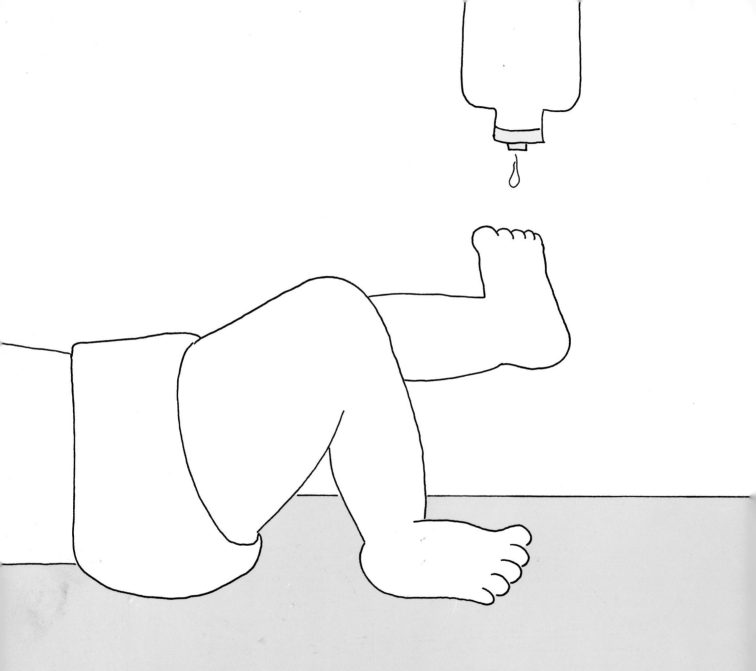

Mama puts lotion on Ruby's toes.

Ruby puts lotion on Ruby's toes.

Mama combs
Ruby's curly hair.

Ruby combs
Ruby's curly hair.

Mama is ready to tuck Ruby in for the night.

But where is Ruby?

Ruby crawls over . . .

and she crawls under.

Ruby helps Daddy read the news.

"Time for bed," Mama says.

But Ruby hides again. Where is she now?

"Time to sleep, Baby Ruby," says Daddy.

But Ruby makes her getaway.

Ruby sits here.

Ruby sits there.

Now Ruby sits beside a mess.

Kitty is sleeping.

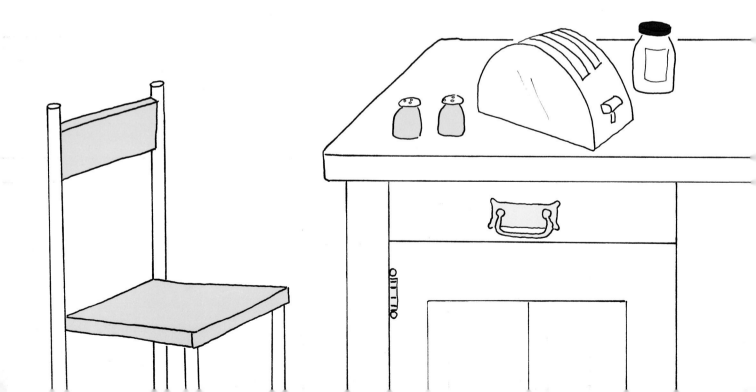

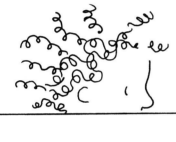

Daddy scoops Ruby up.

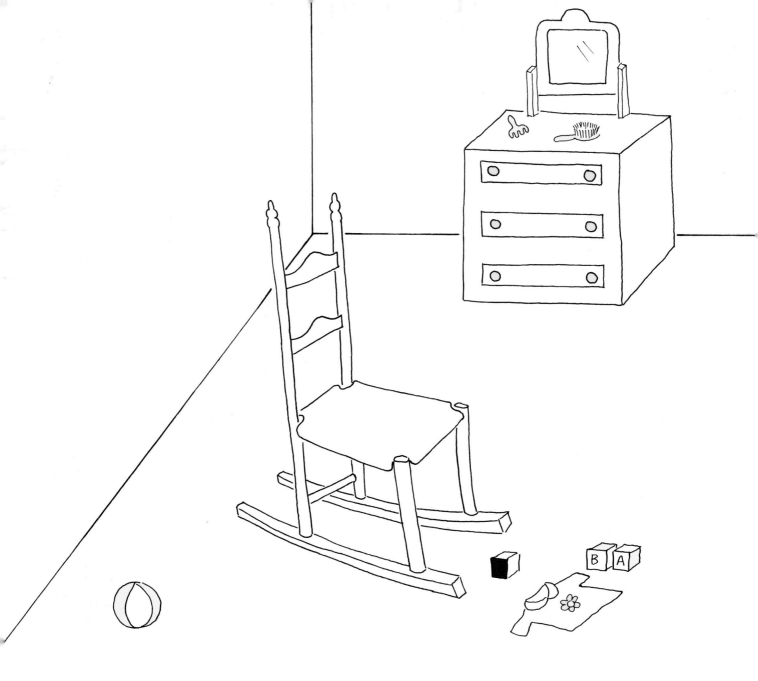

"Good night, Baby Ruby."

Ruby is fast asleep.